# DRAGONBLOOD

# EYE OF THE MONSTER

### BY MICHAEL DAHL

ILLUSTRATED BY

**www.raintreepublishers.co.uk**
Visit our website to find out
more information about
Raintree books.

**To order:**
Phone 0845 6044371
Fax +44 (0) 1865 312263
Email myorders@capstonepub.co.uk

Customers from outside the UK please telephone +44 1865 312262

Raintree is an imprint of Capstone Global Library Limited,
a company incorporated in England and Wales having its
registered office at 7 Pilgrim Street, London,
EC4V 6LB – Registered company number: 6695582

Text © Stone Arch Books 2010
First published in the United Kingdom
in hardback and paperback in 2010

Art Director: Kay Fraser
Graphic Designer: Hilary Wacholz
Production Specialist: Michelle Biedschied
Editor: Vaarunika Dharmapala
Originated by Capstone Global Library Ltd
Printed and bound in China
by South China Printing Company Ltd

ISBN 978 1 406215 24 3 (hardback)
14 13 12 11 10
10 9 8 7 6 5 4 3 2 1

ISBN 978 1 406215 38 0 (paperback)
14 13 12 11 10
10 9 8 7 6 5 4 3 2 1

**British Library Cataloguing in Publication Data**
A full catalogue record for this book is available
from the British Library.

# CONTENTS

# Introduction

A new Age of Dragons is about to begin. The powerful creatures will return to rule the world once more, but this time it will be different. This time, they will have allies who will help them. Around the world, some young humans are making a strange discovery. They are learning that they were born with dragon blood – blood that gives them amazing powers.

CHAPTER 1
**BLOODY**

One NIGHT, a boy named Ren ran through the streets of **Tokyo**.

His nose was **Bloody**

His clothes were **torn**.

A *bruise* darkened his cheek.

Earlier, Ren had walked out of a cinema. He saw some other boys from his school.

The other boys were OLDER and **stronger**. They had hard muscles and cruel smiles.

They laughed because Ren was small and weak.

They **knocked** him around.
They **ripped** his school uniform.

A *fist flew* into Ren's face
and crunched his nose.

**Blood** spattered on to
his shirt.

Harsh laughter echoed in the
street as Ren *ran* for safety.

# CHAPTER 2
# THE REFLECTION

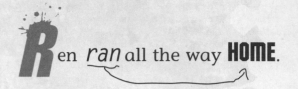

**R**en *ran* all the way **HOME**.

He stopped **OUTSIDE** in the garden to catch his breath.

He **knelt** down by a small pool.

His hands scooped up cold WATER to clean his face.

His hands trembled with anger.

The cold water could not keep his face from feeling *hot*.

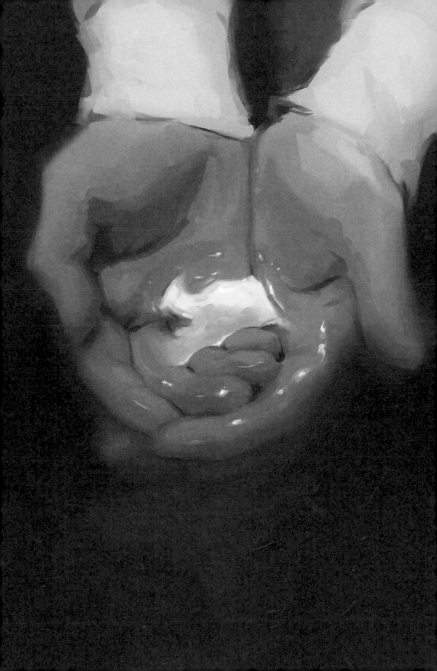

Ren leaned over and **looked** at himself in the pool. Light from a **window** lit his face.

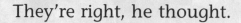

They're right, he thought.

I am **small** and weak.

Why couldn't I be taller?

Why don't I have muscles like theirs?

His nose was swollen. His eyes looked red and full of FEAR

CHAPTER 3
# THE NIGHTMARE

**R**en wiped the **TEARS** from his face. Then he noticed something.

His **eyes** had changed colour.

They were no longer **brown**.

Instead, they looked **HUGE** and golden.

The eyes reminded him of a **nightmare** he'd had many times.

In the *dream*, he turned into a giant black dragon. The nightmare dragon had **burning** yellow eyes.

"That was only a dream," the boy said to himself.

Then he felt a **sharp** pain in his back.

He stared down into the pool.

Two huge black **WINGS** were

sprouting from his shoulders.

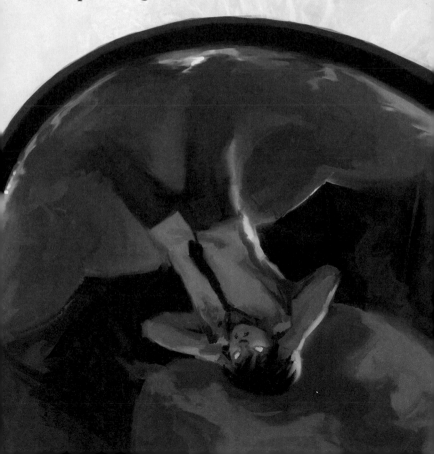

His eyes *gleamed* yellow.

His face turned into the face of a MONSTER. It was fierce and powerful looking. He was terrifying and strong.

"Yes!" shouted the boy.

But the word sounded like a roar coming from his new and massive throat.

Two dark wings **flapped** in the garden. The boy's feet, now armed with sharp **talons**, lifted up from the grass.

The shadowy **CREATURE** turned
and soared above the house.

CHAPTER 4
# THE PREDATOR

A dragon flew above the **bright** streets of Tokyo.

The creature **sniffed** the air. Its yellow eyes scanned the ground, searching for prey.

Four boys laughed and joked as they **walked** down an alley.

A **HUGE** shadow dropped in front of them. The boys **stopped** and stared.

The **powerful** creature reached out a huge claw. It gripped two of the boys within its talons. The boys **SCREAMED.**

Then the dragon leaped into the air. The boys hung below the **MONSTER**, trapped in its grip.

They yelled for **HELP**.

"Now you know how it feels," screamed the dragon. His voice sounded like a fierce **ROAR.**

The dragon flew higher into the evening sky.

Hovering above the CITY,

the dragon bent its head to look at

its prey.

The boys had stopped screaming.

They trembled with FEAR.

The dragon stared into their

faces. It recognized the look in their

eyes. It was a look that the dragon

had seen in its own eyes only

minutes ago.

Swiftly, the creature flew back to the alley. It gently placed the boys on the ground. Then it soared away.

The dragon flew to a quiet garden in a DARK part of the city. It landed near a small pool. Softly, it folded its huge WINGS.

The dragon was a fierce creature, but Ren did NOT want to be a monster.

# IN THE EYE OF THE BEHOLDER

In 1793, a girl with **one** eye in the middle of her forehead was born in France. She lived to be 15.

Eye colour comes from a **pigment** called melanin. Eyes that don't have any melanin are blue. Brown eyes have lots of melanin. In between blue and brown come green, hazel, gold, and sometimes violet eyes.

Most **babies** are born with blue eyes, but eye colour continues to change and develop for a few more years. A person's eye colour is usually set by three years of age. However, eye colour can continue to change due to age or disease as well.

Some people have eyes that are two different colours. This is called heterochromia. Demi Moore, Kiefer Sutherland, and Kate Bosworth are just a few famous people with this condition.

Italian women used to put drops of juice from the poisonous belladonna plant in their eyes to enlarge their pupils. They believed this would make their eyes look brighter, enhancing their beauty.

On the inside corner of your eye is the remnant of a third eyelid. Some animals, such as reptiles, still have this protective lid after their birth.

# ABOUT THE AUTHOR

Michael Dahl is the author of more than 200 books for children and young adults. He has won the AEP Distinguished Achievement Award three times for his non-fiction. His Finnegan Zwake mystery series was shortlisted twice by the Anthony and Agatha awards. He has also written the Library of Doom series. He is a featured speaker at conferences on graphic novels and high-interest books for boys.

# ABOUT THE ILLUSTRATOR

After getting a graphic design degree and working as a designer for a couple of years, Federico Piatti realized he was spending far too much time drawing and painting, and too much money on art books and comics, so his path took a turn towards illustration. He currently works creating imagery for books and games, mostly in the fantasy and horror genres.

# GLOSSARY

**bruise** dark mark you get on your skin when you fall or are hit

**creature** living being

**cruel** mean, happy to see others suffer

**darkened** made darker

**fierce** violent, dangerous, extreme

**harsh** cruel or rough

**muscles** parts of the body that produce movement and show strength

**predator** animal that lives by hunting other animals

**prey** animal that is hunted by other animals

**recognize** see something and know what it is

**sprouting** starting to grow

# DISCUSSION QUESTIONS

**1.** Why were the other boys picking on Ren? What could he have done to stop them?

**2.** Why do you think Ren's eyes changed colour? What other transformations did he go through?

**3.** Why didn't Ren hurt the bullies? What would you have done? Explain your answer.

# WRITING PROMPTS

**1.** Ren doesn't want to be a **bully**. Write about a time when you were bullied. What happened?

**2.** Were you surprised by the ending? Write a paragraph describing what you thought would happen at the end.

**3.** Pick one of the **characters** from the story. Then write one more chapter describing what happened to him.

# MORE BOOKS TO READ

## LIBRARY OF DOOM

Meet the mysterious Librarian. Keeper of the world's most dangerous books, sworn enemy of monsters made of paper and ink, crusader of young people threatened by ancient curses... Enter the Library of Doom to follow these heart-pounding adventures.

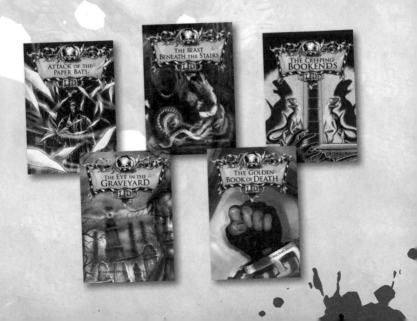